NOW I KNOW HOW!

Demetra Yuvanu

Ages 8–12

Illustrations by Creative Florence

Illustrations by Creative Florence
www.creativeflorence.uk

ISBN 978-0-9840421-1-1

DEMANU BOOKS LLC
August 2017

North America and international (retail and wholesale)
themetra@hotmail.com

This book uses the Dyslexie font,
the typeface for people with dyslexia.
Go to www.dyslexiefont.com to find out
more about the typeface.

This book is dedicated to my two lovely grandchildren.

Luc and Aiden, may you always make wise life choices.
May you focus on kindness and honesty.
May you be happy.

A mysterious dream
A fascinating enigma
A wondrous adventure

Contents

1
Nighttime Under the Covers

The upper house story started one stormy night in Haris' dream. That's where Haris and the peculiar woman first met. She was gorgeous and exciting, wise and childlike, sweet and powerful. Their dream encounter was the beginning of an unusual and dear relationship that carried Haris to places unimaginable.

It was a very loud and turbulent night. The heavy rain was drenching everything. The wind was raging fast and furious, bending the branches on the trees. It was rearranging everything that stood in its way. Mixed sounds of forceful rain and gusty wind were creating a song that was both beautiful and scary. It was that very song that made Haris feel the safety of his warm bed all the way down to his bones. Haris was lying there, very grateful for being indoors and out of all the turmoil. The crackling sounds were growing louder outside his window. The whistling noises made him appreciate the snugness of his bed and all the cozy sensations that it brought up in him.

In the meantime, the leaves outside found themselves here, there, and everywhere. The wind seemed merciless. It was tossing them from one end of the yard to the other. They found themselves against tree trunks, upside-down, or crunched in a pile. They were unrecognizable from their bright looks of a few hours back. Although under the covers, Haris knew exactly what was happening to the leaves. He knew how the wild wind and rain were blasting and destroying them.

Earlier today, the leaves were on their mother tree or on the ground enjoying their outdoor home, Haris thought. *Then this storm came up and changed everything. How fast it all happened! Did they have a warning?* He wondered.

Haris' good friends Alex and Stefan popped into his mind. He had fun with them earlier today. The three boys loved exploring the little town they lived in. That was their favorite pastime. They liked playing all sorts of games while riding their bikes up and down the narrow streets. Sometimes they would pretend they were acrobats in a circus riding on a tightrope. They would draw a long thick line on the sidewalk with chalk and would try to ride very carefully on it. Alex was really good at this game. He could go the width of two houses or more without falling off the chalk line. This imaginary rope act had always been easy for Alex.

Haris, on the other hand, was a poor circus performer. He would shake a lot trying to keep his bike straight. Nothing like Alex, for sure. Most of the time Haris would fall off the line before he got started.

Stefan was not very good at riding the imaginary tight rope

A mysterious dream
A fascinating enigma
A wondrous adventure

either. Haris remembered how sometimes Alex would be at the end of the white chalk line, while he and Stefan lay on top of one another. That's when they looked like the leaves in tonight's storm. Haris, Stefan, and their bikes crunched up in a pile. That image made Haris smile.

Haris pulled the covers over his head wishing hard he could ride the imaginary rope as well as Alex. *I really want to ride the chalk line without falling off,* he thought. *But I always fall off, just can't do it good,* he complained silently.

Haris, Alex and Stefan, had been friends since they were little. The three boys loved to talk. They loved chitchatting about everything and anything that came their way. They talked about what they saw, what they heard, what they imagined, even what they dreamt of.

Listening to the raging weather, Haris kept wondeing about the fate of the leaves. With heavy eyes he was also thinking about Alex and Stefan.

Thoughts of leaves, Alex and Stefan, were tumbling in his mind as he drifted off to sleep. Then he had that exciting but bizarre dream. His peculiar encounter with the strange woman felt very real.

Still Under the Covers

Haris was not sure if all of this had really happened during the previous night. *I never had a dream like that before. It sure was different. I'm not sure if it was happy or a little scary,* he thought with his eyes still closed. He was trying hard not to let the feeling of the dream dissolve in the morning sunlight.

Bright sun rays were pouring through the open bedroom window and onto his eyelids, welcoming him to a new day. Haris didn't know why he had such a mixture of emotions this morning. He only knew it all had to do with his visit with the peculiar woman in the dream.

During his night travel he met a woman who was quite strange. It seemed she appeared into his awareness from nowhere. It almost felt as if she floated out of his body! *How could that be possible,* he wondered in the morning. *I guess dreams are like that sometimes. They don't make any sense when we're awake.*

In the dream the strange woman was looking into his eyes. Her stare made Haris feel a little uncomfortable, but also at ease. He somehow knew that she was aware of everything about him. There was nothing he could hide from her even if he tried. He also knew she could read all his thoughts. They were hers too. In a strange way, Haris was OK with that. It didn't bother him that she knew what was going on in his head.

Stefan and Alex were also part of her awareness. She seemed to know everything about them. Haris was so impressed with her! *She probably knew everything about the whole world! She was the wisest person I ever met. I could trust her too, like I could Alex and Stefan,* Haris thought. *When I was around her last night it was warm and comfy. It felt kinda like my blankets,* he daydreamed some more.

He thought of her glistening hair in the dream's sunlight.

Her big eyes looked like brilliant green marbles. Her exquisite appearance had taken Haris captive. He remembered how graceful she was, talking and moving about. Her shiny red dress with splashes of purple and gold sparkled in the bright light. She wore colorful peacock feathers in her hair that looked like a hat, or a crown of some kind. At times some of them would blow over and cover her lively eyes. Then the breeze would uncover them again. She looked very mysterious then.

Beautiful feathers decorated her sleeves too. Those made her arms look like bird wings. Haris had never seen such exquisite beauty before. Everything about her was fascinating: her dress, her face, her speech, her posture, her movements, her head decoration. Exquisiteness was pouring from her in every way.

The strange lady giggled a lot. She would say something to Haris and then chuckle happily. Haris kept replaying the dream in the privacy of his head while still in bed. There was confusion in his mind about her age though. *I wonder how old she was? She seemed very old and smart,* he thought.

Then he remembered the time she had her finger in her mouth. She was thinking about a question Haris had asked, twirling her finger between her lips like a little girl. *She didn't look much like a grown-up then,* Haris thought.

Haris knew this morning, that from now on, this strange woman was his private and trusting friend. She was the new friendly addition to his life. Awake or asleep, he knew he could contact her. She said so. She would always be there if he needed her. He trusted she would always be loyal and kind.

Haris was still lying in bed thinking of last night. Trying to figure out the feelings of the dream, he decided to give this new friend a name. *What should I call her? What name would fit her best? What if I named her "Joy" because she was so happy all the time,* he wondered. He then remembered when she took his hand and caressed it softly. *Maybe "Love" because she was so loving,* Haris thought silently. *Maybe "Beauty" would be a better name for her,* he wondered some more. All of a sudden he knew the best way to take care of his dilemma! He would give her a name that was very unusual. He was going to call her something unique. He was going to make up a name that spoke of her and only of her. It would describe her in the best way he could imagine.

Haris liked making up new words. He had always enjoyed closing his eyes and seeing letters float and tumble around. Then they would come together and surprise, there was a new word! A word that was just his for a while, until he released it to join the rest of the words in the world.

While thinking of all these possible names, Haris could sense a word taking form in a nebulous way. He knew deeply that it was just a matter of time before he had the right name in front of him. He had a strange sense that he could reach out there somewhere and grab the nebulous name with his mind. If only he could see it a little more clearly in his mind's eye! He then could say it out loudly and the name wouldn't be nebulous any more.

Then abruptly, as if someone invisible put the word together, he had his answer! No more dilemma about her name. It would be a combination of all that she was to him. He would call her "BeJoWiLo." "Be" stood for beautiful. "Jo" was short for joyful. "Wi" was for wise. "Lo" was half of the word love because she was so very lovable and loving.

"BeJoWiLo," he said in a low voice and smiled. Haris really liked the way it made his mouth, his ears, and his heart feel when he repeated over and over, "BeJoWiLo, BeJoWiLo."

His mother's voice brought him back into the room, taking him away from daydreaming. The reality of the morning routine was here once more. There was no school today. It was spring vacation. Haris could spend most of this warm day with Stefan and Alex. He loved being with his two friends. They always had lots of fun together.

Maybe we'll go exploring again, he thought.

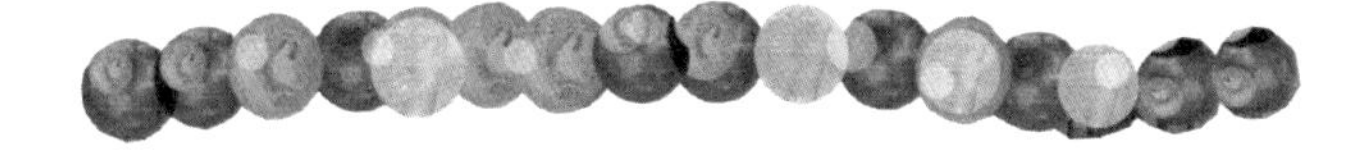

3

Playtime

"I'm up Mom," he said loudly, jumping out of bed. The sun was already on its way toward the middle of the sky. It was bathing with warmth everything that had been battered in last night's storm. The leaves were gleaming in the clear daylight, getting drier and warmer. *How nice that must feel to them,* Haris thought and smiled. *It probably feels the same like after I get wet playing in the sprinkler and the sun warms me up. It feels so good, and my body looks funny with all the goose bumps on it.*

He had almost finished his breakfast when he heard his two friends coming up to the house. He jumped up, dropping the last of the toast in his dog's mouth.

"I'll be right out," he shouted, tripping over Kiko's tail. "Kiko, look out. Let me by!" he said, pushing the black puppy gently out of his way.

His mom gave Kiko to him last month on his tenth birthday. Kiko looked like an oval watermelon covered with black fur. His face was hardly visible under the hairy forest. Somewhere in there were a nose, two eyes and a mouth for sure. Kiko inhaled all his food with loud and frantic gulps. *You sure are cute Kiko,* Haris thought, opening the door. He pushed it wide open and ran out.

"Hi Stefan, hi Alex," he greeted his friends. Then he ran to the side of the house to get his bike.

"Hi Haris," the two said back almost at the same time.

"Where you wanna go today?" asked Alex.

"Let's go to that path behind Mrs. Timber's house," said Stefan.

They agreed with Stefan's idea and off they went. They rode one behind the other like ducklings following the invisible mother duck, queen of adventure and excitement. The bikes were making sometimes visible and sometimes invisible wavy paths on the ground that resembled snakes. The long imaginary reptiles had their heads back at Haris' front yard. Their bodies stretched and got longer as the boys rode leisurely toward their destination.

"Let's play the circus act real quick," said Alex, getting a big piece of chalk out of his pocket.

"OK," said Haris. "I hope I can do it better today."

"Me too. Alex, draw the line over there in front of Mr. Jake's house," said Stefan.

Alex jumped off his bike, put it down and drew a long chalk line on the sidewalk. It started at Mr. Jake's and ended at the end of Mrs. Martin's house.

"Who's going first?" asked Haris.

"I'll go," said Alex. He rode like a perfect circus performer. He stayed on the chalk line without straying. *He did it again,* Haris thought.

Stefan and Haris tried, but ended up straying more than riding the fake rope.

"I don't want to play this anymore today," said Haris. *I wish I could do this like Alex,* he thought.

"C'mon, let's ride to the path," said Stefan, ready to move on to the next activity of the day.

Riding under the trees, the birds were flying circles around them. Then, they would fly back around the trees that had been their home for the night.

"I really like these little guys," said Stefan. Once in a while one of them would fly close to their heads or faces as if to amuse them with a quick kiss. Haris, Stefan, and Alex loved the way the tiny birds were bouncing all over. They were making big swipes toward the ground and zigzag patterns into the air, chirping cheerfully all the while.

"They're having a good time!" said Haris.

"There's some kind of party going on," said Stefan.

The imaginary snake kept stretching as they approached Mrs. Timber's house. The three friends had taken the path behind the nice lady's house many times. They had always enjoyed their undisturbed playtime back there. The path had a specialness to it. It was different from all the other paths in town. It was quiet and serene, yet so jubilant, with little bursts of sound and movement. It seemed as if trees, plants, and all things alive back there, greeted the boys with jubilance each time they arrived.

They saw Mrs. Timber in her front yard on her knees, planting baby flowers into the dark soil. She raised her hand and greeted them. Her voice was filled with kindness.

"Have fun back there," she said, then looked back down and continued framing the flowerbed with the colorful bunches.

When they entered the path, all of nature was celebrating their arrival. What a welcoming affair! They were off their bikes, walking leisurely and looking at all that was around. Their eyes were searching for sticks and stones with odd shapes. All three had a collection of rocks and little branches with interesting figures and colors. They loved gathering them during their bike rides around town.

Stefan found a stick once which resembled a small airplane. It even had a section in the back that curved upward resembling a plane's tail. His dad hung it from the ceiling over his bed from a long piece of dental floss. Stefan liked lying with his hands under his head looking at it. It was really fun when the breeze through the open window pushed it into flight.

The three friends were walking and searching when Haris yelled out,

"Look, look what I found! A rock that looks like a foot!" Haris put his find on his left palm so they could analyze it better. They all agreed it looked like a human foot.

"The round part back here is like the heel of a foot! And look at the front! It looks like our toes, but there are only four," said Alex.

"That's still like a foot. There are people with only four toes you know," replied Haris. *I want to give it a name,* he thought. In a few minutes he knew what he was going to call the little rock. *I'm going to call it "Littlefourtoe"* he decided silently. Haris was very satisfied with his choice. This was his second new word today.

"Let me introduce you to 'Littlefourtoe' guys," he said.

"Cool name," said Stefan. "Pass 'Littlefourtoe' around so we can touch it too." They were passing Haris' new discovery back and forth comparing its likeness to their own feet. Suddenly, Alex looked up and pointed to something barely visible in the distance.

"What's that out there?" he said, trying to see between the tree branches.

"It looks like part of a building," said Stefan. He was jumping up and down getting short glimpses of it on his way up off the ground. "It looks like ... like... like... a door, or something like that," he said. The sound of the word "door" made Haris extremely curious.

"What are you two seeing over there?" Haris said, tipping his head left and right trying to find out what this was all about. "Guys, I think you're right. It looks like a door..., maybe two..., or... three," he said. *That must be what BeJoWiLo talked about last night,* he thought.

"This is so strange!" said Alex. "Were these doors out there the last time we were here?" he asked.

"I don't think so," replied Stefan in a doubtful voice.

"Yes, I think they were here," said Haris in a voice that made the two believe that he knew something more than they did. "I think they've been here forever; it's just that we were not ready to see them yet. They didn't show themselves to us earlier."

"What are you saying, Haris? How can doors show themselves or not? I don't understand," said Stefan.

"I'll tell you all about this," said Haris, recalling part of what BeJoWiLo told him in the dream. "Let's sit down somewhere," he said.

"OK," said Stefan pointing to some flat rocks. "Let's go over there. I can't wait to hear about this!"

Haris Tells All

The three friends ran to the smooth rocks and sat down. Haris told them everything he could remember about his dream. He talked for a long time. He was moving his whole body trying to describe BeJoWiLo as best he could. He talked about how he felt being around her and how radiant she looked.

Haris also remembered her saying that they would meet again. BeJoWiLo also mentioned something about three doors during last night's dream. She said they were very important. A gift to all that wanted it. The doors could really help Haris, and anyone else who wanted to learn from them. The peculiar thing about them, BeJoWiLo said, was that everyone could not see them. Only someone who was ready to receive the gifts could know they were there.

"This sounds way too crazy," said Alex. "Are we ready now to learn something? Are we ready for some gifts? Maybe that explains why we can see them today and not all the other times we were out here. What do you think we're ready to learn?" he asked his friends and himself.

"I wish I could tell you, Alex," answered Haris. "I don't remember what she said was behind them."

"I'm a little scared to go closer," said Stefan. "Are you sure Haris it's OK to find out what's behind them?" he continued with a frown.

"Well, we're all curious, and I trust BeJoWiLo, so I say we find out," Haris replied. "C'mon, let's do it!"

5
One More Appearance

When Haris said all that he could remember of the dream, Stefan and Alex felt as if they knew BeJoWiLo too.

"I only wish I could meet her too," said Alex.

"I'd like to really know what she looked like," said Stefan.

"I have an idea!" whispered Haris leaning toward them and looking directly into their eyes. "Close your eyes", he said. "Who knows, maybe you'll be able to see her too somehow!" Stefan and Alex liked Haris' suggestion.

"I think that's a neat idea," said Alex, "but I don't think anything will happen."

The two friends were sitting on the flat rocks, eyes closed. Haris was standing now, hands on his knees leaning towards them. They were all hoping that she might appear to Stefan and Alex, the same way she had to Haris in the dream.

"Please, BeJoWiLo," they were both saying in a very low voice. "Please, let us see you."

Haris was watching his friends' faces, anticipating changes in their mouths. *I'll know it right away if she comes to them,* he thought, *because they will probably start smiling.* He was staring at both of them intensely, waiting and wishing too. Then he noticed the corners of their lips starting to move. The edges of their mouths formed a wee smile that continued to grow. The faint smile got bigger until it turned into a loud happy scream.

"We saw her! We saw her!" they both said at once.

"She came to us too! She was just like you told us, Haris. She looked like a kid, kinda like us," blurted out Stefan with excitement.

"She reminded me of my grandma a little too," continued Alex.

"What did she say? What did she do?" asked Haris as he jumped off the rock. "C'mon guys tell me," he shouted bouncing up and down like a rubber ball.

"It was just like watching a movie. She was sort of blurry at first and then she started getting clearer. She was smiling, just standing there," answered Stefan.

"It was different for me," added Alex. "She floated into my movie screen from the left, then stopped in the middle. Then she stood in front of me and opened her arms wide." Alex kept on talking fast. "She then moved closer. It felt like she was hugging me but without really closing her arms. It was so weird but it felt so good too. It was like when my mom hugs me. I can still see her smile and her eyes. They were friendly and kind," Alex said finishing his impressions of BeJoWiLo's visit.

The three friends were excited and puzzled with all these happenings. All three had met BeJoWiLo in different ways. They agreed that from now on BeJoWiLo was going to be their good friend.

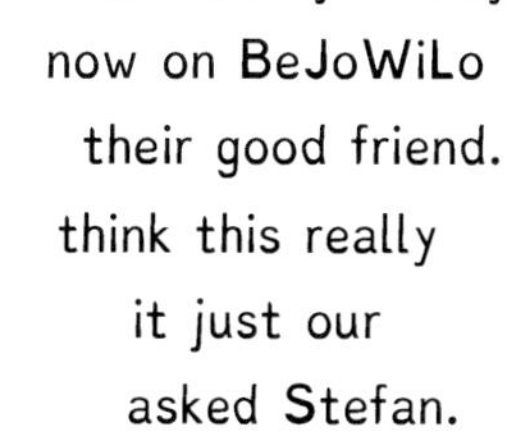

"Haris, do you think this really happened, or was it just our imagination?" asked Stefan.

"Well, you saw her, didn't you?" answered Haris. "Our imagination is sort of like our dreams anyway. It seems real and it happens in our heads. It is still part of us. That's how BeJoWiLo explained it to me in the dream last night."

"So maybe it is real then," said Alex raising his shoulders, not so sure about his own answer.

Haris noticed that Stefan was deep in thought. It was clear to him that he was trying to figure all this out.

"OK, I think I got it," Stefan said. "I'm imagining a cold glass of lemonade right now. M...m...m..., it looks good and I'm getting very thirsty just thinking about it," Stefan continued. "Is that what you meant Haris?" he asked.

"Yeah, I think so. You just imagined the lemonade and boom! It made you thirsty. Was the lemonade real? Maybe it was, in some strange way," said Haris.

"Real or not, I just know how thirsty I am," said Stefan.

"How about some water?" asked Alex pointing to the spring in the distance. The spring was inviting them deeper into the path. The sparkling water was flowing steadily. Its smooth sound was like a promise to Haris, Stefan and Alex. A tempting promise for some fun. They ran to the spring pushing their bikes. They drank the crisp water using their palms for cups. When they were not thirsty anymore, they started getting their arms and heads wet. The sun sparkled on their wet skin as they were splashing water on it.

"Alex, you look like Kiko when he's wet," said Haris looking at Alex shaking the water out of his head.
They all started laughing, shaking their heads, imitating Kiko's crazy moves. After shaking the water off, they picked up their bikes and started on a fast walk to the mystery doors.

6
Anticipation

By now, their curiosity about the doors was like an overblown balloon about to explode. Suspense and anticipation were gradually speeding up their walk. When they couldn't walk any faster they climbed on their bikes and pedaled with force. But the way to the mysterious location was not easy any more. It started turning hard past the spring. The breeze now felt warm as it danced all around them. They pushed hard on the pedals but didn't get very far. Last night's storm had made this part of the path challenging. Rocks had rolled onto it, slowing them down. They had to swerve around them. Broken tree branches were adding to the difficulty.

"I wish all these branches were not in our way," said Alex getting off his bike. He then moved the obstacles to the side, clearing the path for everyone. The three continued riding and stopping, getting on and off their bikes. They were taking turns moving the obstacles out of the way. Haris, Stefan, and Alex had never felt anxious while in this path. Today was a little different. Trying to get to the doors as fast as possible was making them anxious.

I wish the path was a little cleaner. If it wasn't for all these rocks and sticks, we would be there by now. I can't wait to find out what's behind the doors, thought Haris.

The mysterious doors were partly hidden by the foliage of the overgrown path. Their size was not totally obvious to them yet. They seemed to be hanging from the air, not quite touching the ground. They were colorful and seemed to be rectangular in shape.

This is so weird, thought Haris leaning his head forward trying to see better. *This is the strangest thing,* thought Stefan as he looked at Haris with amazement painted all over his face.

The boys looked at one another with puzzled faces. They continued the rest of the way in silence. That was something they didn't do often. There were no words left to describe what was going on. They finally arrived.

7

The First Mystery

Standing outside the first door, they put the bikes down on the damp ground. BeJoWiLo came to their thoughts. She made her appearance in all three minds at the same time. Haris, Stefan, and Alex, smiled to one another and walked closer to the first door. They put all six hands on it. After a short hesitation they pushed. The heavy metal door started moving away slowly. They stood at the opening for a minute and looked at each other in awe. They finally knew what was back there. But they were surprised at what they saw. All their fears connected with the doors were erased in an instant.

"What a relief!" said Stefan exhaling a big sigh. "I had all these scary pictures in my head."

"Wow! What a nice surprise," said Haris.

The wide-open entrance was calling them in. They entered side by side, letting the heavy door close behind them. An explosion of bright colors from the flowers welcomed them.

Haris recalled another part of the dream. He remembered BeJoWiLo talking about different lands.

"Aha! This must be the land of 'beauty' guys. Everything in here is great," Haris said. He knew Stefan and Alex were happy. He could see it in their cheeks. They looked like puffed up little balloons as they smiled.

"What a cool place!" said Alex spinning with his arms spread out, admiring what he was seeing.

"I think I could stay here forever," said Stefan with excitement. "Well..., maybe not really forever, but for a long time anyway," he added.

"Listen!" said Haris. "I'm hearing music.... Where is it coming from? It's spreading all around, coming out of everything!"

The music was traveling around them. Happy sounds were

creating circles around the land of "beauty." Musical notes were flying out of blossoms and trees. Birds and butterflies were joining in the festivity, flapping their wings. They were dancing from flower to flower, adding happiness and magnificence to the show. All this was such a wondrous spectacle! The dance of sound and vivid colors was breathtaking. Leaves and blooms were brighter and fresher after last night's chilly rain. Haris, Stefan, and Alex had not seen such a parade of magnificence before. They were standing on a soft pile of multicolored flower petals in awe at what they were seeing.

"I can't believe this is happening," said Stefan, picking up glistening petals and throwing them into the air. Haris and Alex joined in. Tossing the feathery petals up high over their heads, they were enjoying their soft caresses on their way down. The beauty of the land had captured their senses.

"Something strange is happening here," said Haris shifting his attention to different parts of the land. The longer he looked and admired an area, the more magnificent it became.

"Do you see what I see?" he asked.

"Yeah, I see what you mean," said Alex. "When we pay a lot of attention to something in here, it becomes more beautiful."

The more they admired the colors and sweet smell of the flowers, the brighter they became, sending out a stronger aroma. Focusing their attention on them made them grow and multiply. Noticing their beauty brought about more beautiful changes.

"BeJoWiLo talked about this last night," said Haris. "She said that focusing on something makes more of it."

"I'm not sure I understand what 'focus' means. What did

she say it means?" said Stefan.

"It's like paying attention or something like that, right?" said Alex.

"BeJoWiLo said, '...When we notice something, talk about it, think about it, pay attention to it with our minds or our actions, that's focusing. And when we focus on something, it changes. It changes into more of it.' That's what I remember her saying," said Haris.

"Oh!" said Alex. "So that's what's happening now. We're focusing on all the pretty things in here, and everything is turning more beautiful. This is like magic!"

Stefan started singing, "I'm happy, I'm happy in the land of magic.... In the land of happy, I'm magic, I'm magic..."

"Did you just make that up?" asked Haris.

"Yep," said Stefan kept singing.

"I'm happy, I'm happy in the
land of magic.... In the land of
happy, I'm magic, I'm magic...,"
Haris and Alex joined him.

Three bubbly voices were sending out lots of cheer with their song. The more they sang the happier they got. Singing the song made them feel like magicians. Powerful, happy little magicians. Filled with awe, they walked through the land stepping on velvety beds of color. They sang, laughed and had a wonderful time.

"It's hard to leave here, but I want to see what's behind the second door," said Haris.

"I don't want to go yet," said Stefan.

"I don't either, but I want to see what's hiding behind the rest of them," said Haris, and started walking toward the door.

"OK, let's go. I'm pretty sure we can come back," replied Stefan, curious himself about the rest of the mystery.

"Bye for now pretty land," said Haris. They opened the metal door and walked out.

8

The Second Mystery

Curiosity was speeding up their pace. In no time, they were standing outside the second piece of the three-door puzzle. Without hesitation this time, they put their hands on the door and pushed hard. The anticipation fizzled as the door opened, but the mystery remained when they took a peek inside.

"What's all this?" said Alex and his mouth dropped.

"I'm ready to go back to the first land again," said Stefan.

"Let's check it out you two," said Haris and took a small step inside.

Stefan and Alex stepped in slowly, following him. They let go of the door.

"This must be 'yukland', the land of ugly stuff," said Haris.

"Watch where you step!" said Alex as he grabbed Haris who was about to fall into a mudhole.

"Boy, I almost turned into a mudcicle. You saved me Alex," said Haris.

"This is the land of dark colors and mud," said Stefan. "There's nothing growing in here."

Their eyes were searching for some color other than brown, gray or black, but without any success. Very cautiously they walked around. This place was not fun at all. There were no birds on the dry and crackly trees, no flowers, green leaves, or pleasant smells. There was an irritating humming sound coming out of the earth. They looked at one another in disbelief. It was hard to believe how drab and dreary this place was. The boys had never seen anything as cheerless as this.

"What's this sound?" asked Alex.

"Whatever it is, I don't like it," said Haris, putting his hands over his ears.

"I don't understand what the gift is in this land. What's to learn in here?" Stefan asked.

They looked up at the trees and wondered how they could be so dark and unattractive.

"Look what's happening!" said Haris, pointing at the tree branches. "They're getting cracklier..., they're breaking off...," he said with disbelief.

Lifeless branches were barely hanging from the trees, then dropping loudly to the muddy ground as the boys stood close to each other in complete amazement.

"Is the mud getting thicker? Is it spreading too?" asked Stefan. They were standing on a small rock away from the falling branches.

The noisy activity had pulled them under its spell. Focusing on the happenings made the branches break and tumble to the ground faster and more forcefully. The same was happening with the mud. The more they stared at it, the more it spread.

"We need to get out of here and fast," said Stefan.

"That humming is bothering me. I think it's getting louder too!" said Haris.

They jumped off the rock. Running as fast as they could, they were splashing mud all over themselves and one another. They wove their way carefully through the unattractive land trying to stay away from the trees. With mud-heavy shoes and out of breath they made it back to the door. They pulled it open with all their strength and dashed out.

"That was something else!" said Stefan, wiping off his face with his sleeves.

"I thought this door was going to be as nice as the first," said Alex, knocking mud off his shoes with a small stick.

"You know what I'm thinking?" said Haris. "I'm thinking

that both doors were kinda the same."

"Are you crazy?" shouted Stefan. "It was so pretty in the first one, how were they the same?"

"I said, kinda the same," answered Haris. "What was back of them was different all right. I'm talking about the way things were changing," Haris continued.

"Oh, I think I know what you're saying," said Alex. "In both lands, changes happened in a jiffy. We focused and boom, it happened. We talked about the flowers and they got more beautiful. We stared at the mud and it started spreading. We complained about the humming, and it got worse."

They looked at one another, eyes filled with questions. There were no clear answers. They still didn't understand what all this meant. They only knew that behind both doors, it was their focus that made things change.

"We have one more to check out," said Haris.

"I hope it's not like the last one," said Stefan, and followed his friends.

9

The Third Mystery

The third door was now completely visible. A few more steps and the rest of this mystery would dissolve.

"Ready?" asked Haris when they got there. They spread all thirty muddy fingers on the cool metal door.

"One, two, three, push!" said Alex.

The door flung open but the riddle remained unsolved once more.

"What do you make of this?" said Stefan.

"I don't know. I just know it's weird again," said Alex.

"BeJoWiLo said some things last night about 'choosing'," said Haris. "She said the choice to pick between things was ours. This is the last door, so we must be in the land of 'choice' then. The land where we get to choose something, but what?" Haris went on.

Hoping to solve the puzzle, they entered all the way. Once again they were presented with a riddle. This land's mystery was more complicated though. It was made out of all the things that were present in the two previous lands; out of the beautiful and the not so beautiful. A land made out of charm and yuk side by side.

"This is so crazy," said Alex.

"Pretty things and ugly things side by side," said Haris. "Look how huge these flowers are!" he said pointing at a bush packed with red blooms.

With everyone's attention focused on them, the red blooms started multiplying and turning a brighter red. The aroma streaming from them was bathing the three friends, putting smiles of pleasure on their faces once more. They stood in place absorbed by the beauty, as cheerful music was spreading all around.

"The land of 'beauty' is taking over!" shouted Haris.

"Yeah, look at the plants spreading over the mud! The

music is taking over the humming too!" said Stefan.

When they first entered they could see both lands. Now, one of them was magically fading away. The boys were mesmerized. Shrinking slowly out of sight, the ugly was yielding to the beautiful.

"This is unreal!" said Alex, dancing around.
Music was bouncing off trees and plants once more. The more they loved being there, the prettier it all became.

"I think an invisible giant mouth is swallowing the land of 'ugly'," said Haris all excited.

"I can still see a little of it over there, it's not gone all the way yet," said Stefan, pointing at some dry branches. "I hope the giant mouth swallows the ugly land fast."

"I don't want any part of that second land again," said Alex frowning.

Before they knew it, the boys were talking about the second door again, and how much they disliked it back there. Their attention was drifting to what they didn't want. Their shift from admiring the beautiful land to dreading the ugly one happened fast. Their change of focus made their favorite land practically dissolve in front of them. They stood in amazement, dreading being there.

"Oh no, not again!" said Alex, seeing the return of "yukland."

"It's coming back quick! It's taking over everything!" said Haris with an alarmed voice.
Complaining and protesting made things worse. It was like pouring gasoline on a fire. The fire was "yukland." what they didn't want, and the gasoline was all the dreading and complaining.

The colorful scenery was almost replaced by the dreaded sight when Haris remembered BeJoWiLo's words. During the dream, feathers blowing over her eyes, she said,

"...Don't forget, you have a choice. You can choose to change your focus. You can put it on what you want, and take it away from what you don't want."

"I'm pretty sure we're in the land of 'choice', guys," Haris said fast but with very little enthusiasm. "Let's try what BeJoWiLo said. If we choose to put our attention on the pretty land, maybe we can bring it back. Let's try it!"

"And how do we do that?" asked Stefan.

"We'll change our attention," Haris replied. "Let's do it now before it gets harder."

Standing on top of a rock away from the mud, one more time they turned their heads toward what was left of the pretty land. They had agreed to change their focus, so they kept all six eyes on the fading land of 'beauty'.

It was not hard to become captives of such beauty once again. Admiration and excitement for the land returned fast. With it returned the strong aroma, the cheerful music, and the brilliant colors. Softly but steadily their shift of attention brought the first land back in sight. Their choice to focus at what they loved, instead of what they dreaded, worked.

They found themselves exactly where they wanted to be, in the land of attractive things again. They sang, hopped around and laughed in the land of their choice into the early afternoon. Haris, Stefan, and Alex were very excited with their achievement. Lost fully in their adventure, they ignored their growling stomachs. Not for long though, since the growling demanded to be silenced.

"We have to leave guys," said Haris. "I'm really hungry."

"I hate to go, but I'm hungry too," said Stefan putting both hands over his stomach.

They skipped their way back to the entrance very hungry and very happy. They grabbed the metal handle and pulled.

"We have to come back," said Alex, passing through the opening.

"Now we know what to do if 'yukland' shows up again. Let's bring our lunch next time," said Stefan.

"Good idea!" said Haris.

10
The Understanding

The third land was behind the closed door now. They ran to their bikes, hopped on and started back up the path. With the rocks already pushed out of the way and the mud a little drier, the ride back was easier.

The adventurous morning behind them, they tried to figure out what it all meant. What were the lessons and the gifts BeJoWiLo had talked about in the dream?

"Haris, what do you think BeJoWiLo was talking about?" asked Alex. "Let's see..., what did we learn?"

"Well..., I just remembered some more," answered Haris. "Behind the doors there was no time. Everything happened in a flash. She said that when we're back out here, things happen slower. That's why we have to be patient. We can practice what we learned, except for this time thing," he added, scratching the top of his head.

"You mean we can choose what we want, focus on it and make it happen?" asked Stefan.

The dream was returning to Haris' mind a piece at a time.

"Well... yes, but not that fast, I don't think," Haris replied. "She said we shouldn't forget that things take more time in the world outside of the doors."

"That's still cool, even if we have to wait some," said Alex. "We have to try it, see how it works out here too."

Haris could sense another part of the dream becoming clear.

"She also said that out here in our world, sometimes focusing had to have some doing with it," Haris said, trying to explain BeJoWiLo's words.

"Explain, explain," said Alex.

"I'm trying, I'm trying," said Haris. "What I understood was that in our world sometimes 'focusing' also means 'doing.'

Behind the doors we didn't have to take any action and we didn't have to wait before we saw things change. Back there 'focusing' meant putting attention only with our minds. BeJoWiLo said that out here very often putting attention means taking action."

By now, Mrs. Timber's flowerbed was filled with the colorful tiny plants. She was done working in it. She spent the morning focusing on making it pretty. She put all her attention on digging and planting.

Mrs. Timber loved putting the little plants in their new home. She talked to them lovingly, making sure each of them was in their best spot. Now she had to wait for them to grow.

Had Mrs. Timber met BeJoWiLo too and learned her lessons? Maybe she has her own BeJoWiLo, with a different name of course, Haris thought. Then he said,

"Mrs. Timber focused on her flower bed with her mind and she did something too. Her action was to dig and plant. That's what BeJoWiLo meant," he continued, trying to make sense of it all.

Following the same route back to Haris' house, they passed the white chalk line in front of Mr. Jake's and Mrs. Martin's. Haris looked at the line and whined to himself silently, *I can never ride this stupid line straight; I always fall off of it.*

Suddenly he thought of the lessons. Behind the doors he had learned what happens when you put attention on what you want. And what he wanted was to ride the chalk line as well as Alex. He decided right there and then, not to focus any longer on how he kept falling off. That would be the same as when he focused on the mud. Things would only get worse that way. And he didn't want that. What he wanted was to get better at this game.

I'm not going to even think about falling off anymore, he told himself silently. No more fussing and complaining. From now on, Haris was going to put his attention on riding the chalk line as straight as Alex. He was going to put all his focus on perfecting his circus act. He was going to put time into becoming good at it. *That's it*, he thought, *I'll focus on riding straight and I'll do it.*

"You know what?" Haris said with excitement to his buddies. "I know how I'm gonna use that 'focusing' lesson we learned back there. I'm gonna get good at riding the chalk line." Haris noticed Stefan smiling. He knew that he was also going to focus on riding straight. Haris could tell by the spark in his friend's eyes.

Alex was listening quietly. Haris knew that Alex was also searching quietly for something to change, something to focus on, and make it different. Haris saw him smile too. *He's gonna put attention on something too, I can tell. But I don't know what?* he thought, because Alex didn't say anything.

All three, rode back together until they got to Haris' street. Then they separated.

"Bye, guys," said Haris heading to his house.

"Bye, see you later," said Alex.

"See you guys," added Stefan.

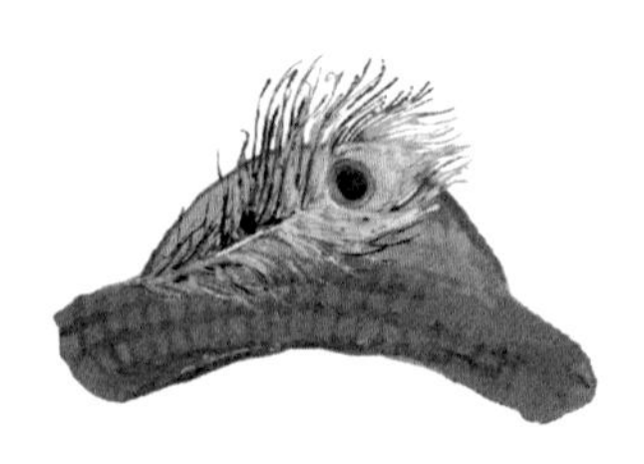

11

The Doing

Kiko greeted Haris at the door. His tail flopping left and right as the four-legged friend followed his two-legged buddy into the kitchen.

"Hey Kiko, do you have a little tail motor under all that hair?" Haris said. "C'mon boy let's eat, cause I have work to do after lunch."

Haris was especially hungry that day. He ate all his lunch, except for a few grapes. He tossed those to Kiko one by one. Kiko, the furry watermelon, loved grapes. He waited with an open mouth as Haris threw them like basketballs through a hoop.

"Let's shoot one more basket Kiko," he said, aiming one more grape at the pretend basketball hoop.
Kiko caught the juicy grape once more, just as he had every other time. Haris had never missed a basket playing with Kiko, his mobile hoop.

After lunch, Kiko and Haris went outside. Haris decided to use the long cement walkway on the side of the house as his practice area.

"This is exactly what I need," he said all excited, circling a thick piece of chalk between his fingers. "Kiko, my faithful companion, you're gonna be my audience. Circus performers need an audience, you know."

Haris drew three long chalk lines the length of the cemented area. He drew them as close together as he could, then filled in the gaps where the lines didn't touch. That made one wide chalk line ready for action.

BeJoWiLo where are you? I want you to help me do this, he thought and sat down by his bike. He closed his eyes for a minute. She made her smiling appearance in his mind's eye. Just as she promised, she was there for him. They connected in Haris' mind and her suggestions turned into Haris' thoughts.

You can focus on this a little easier, if you break it up into smaller parts, she said through his thoughts.
It took a couple of minutes for Haris to understand what she meant. Then he got it. *I'll break up the line into two smaller lines! I'll practice riding only half of the way first,* he thought. He walked to about the middle of the chalk line and marked a small circle on it. For today he was going to focus riding only to the circle. Tomorrow he would try the whole length of the imaginary rope. *BeJoWiLo had the right idea. That sounds easier than doing it all at the same time,* he thought and smiled.

He stood up, got on the bike and started down the imaginary rope, but so did Kiko. He kept running in front of Haris making it harder for him to keep his balance.

That's not gonna work, Haris thought and put down the bike. He picked up Kiko and walked to the old tree next to his practice area. The cloth hammock hanging from it was a great solution to Haris' problem. He put Kiko in the hanging bed and ran into the kitchen. He came back with a couple of dog biscuits in hand.

"These will keep you happy and out of the way," he said, and put the dog snacks in the hammock.
Kiko took one in his mouth and looked at his playmate with thankful eyes. Haris gave the big colorful swing a gentle push, and walked back to his bike.

His entire focus this afternoon would be on practicing. All his attention would be on perfecting the pretend circus act. He could sense BeJoWiLo's presence. It made him feel powerful and capable. He rode some, wobbled a lot, and jumped off many times. He did this over and over, while his thoughts stayed focused on getting good and not on falling off the line. *I can do this; I'm good at it. I can do this; I'm good at it,* he kept repeating silently.

Haris was concentrating only on what he wanted, just as he did behind the third door. And what he wanted was to ride on the line without wobbling or falling off. He made the choice to ride well and he was concentrating on that choice. Little by little, the wobbling started to lessen. As the afternoon went on, Haris was jumping off less and riding more. He was thrilled with his improvement. Kiko's lively bark reminded Haris it was time to quit for the day.

"We'll do this again early tomorrow morning Kiko," he said, leaning the bike against the house. He then climbed into the hammock with the furry watermelon. Haris and his shaggy pal

I choose.
I focus.
I make it happen!

stayed in there swinging for some time.

It wasn't long after Haris finished dinner that night, that he got ready for bed. He wanted to get enough sleep and be well rested for the morning practice. He set his alarm clock one hour earlier than usual and crawled under the covers. The day's events had tired him very much, so he fell asleep right away.

Early the next two mornings, everyone still asleep, even Kiko, Haris went out to the side of the house and picked up where he had left off the day before. He got back on his bike and rode to the halfway mark. He rode with enthusiasm, thrilled with the thought of Alex' and Stefan's surprised faces when they'd see what he had accomplished. He kept riding up to the marked circle, knowing that he needed just a little more time before he mastered his act. Haris knew now how things change when you focus on them. The other day he saw changes happen instantly behind the doors. He saw flowers multiply, and mud get thicker. He saw exquisite beauty change into unattractive things, and back to exquisite magnificence again. But out here away from the doors, it took a little more time for changes to happen.

This is working, he thought and kept riding better and better. By the second morning he could ride steadily to the halfway mark without wobbling.

I think I'm ready for the second half today, he thought, putting his foot on the right pedal. *I can ride halfway good; I can ride all the way good. I can ride halfway good; I can ride all the way good,* he was saying silently over and over. He pushed on one pedal, lifted his opposite foot onto the other pedal, and off he went. He started down the white chalk line with great confidence. Certain today that before the morning was over, he would ride steadily all the way. And he did, but it happened much sooner than he expected. He got to the end without wavering after only three attempts. He accomplished the entire circus act with enormous trust in himself. Even so, he was a little surprised it all happened so fast.

BeJoWiLo, how come I didn't have to practice a lot on the second half? he asked without moving his lips. Her answer merged with his thoughts. He could hear her kind response through his own thinking once more.

It was your decision Haris to change your riding that made things easier for you. When you decided to focus with your mind and your actions, I was there to support you and speed things up, she said.

"BeJoWiLo is full of neat ways to do stuff," Haris said. His happy words spread out into the morning air.

12

Circus Fun

Alex and Stefan were coming over later that morning. Haris could hardly wait for the show and tell. Knowing they would be impressed with his achievement made him feel good inside. He had just finished with breakfast when Stefan and Alex showed up.

"Haaaaris..., guess what came to town last night!" he heard Stefan's loud voice.

"I know," said Haris, opening the kitchen door. "The circus! And we're all going this afternoon. Surpriiiise!"

"We are?" Stefan and Alex asked in one breath.

"Yes, all together," said Haris and ran out to meet his friends. "My mom already bought tickets for all of us. She just told me she talked to your mom, and your mom, already," he said pointing first at Stefan, then at Alex.

"Guess what?" said Stefan. "I can ride good now. I did what BeJoWiLo said and it worked."

I knew he'd do that, thought Haris.

"Well..., same here," he said. "I can too. Let's go do it."

They went to Haris' practice area and did what all three now knew how to do very well. Up and down the chalk line they rode with certainty and joy. After a while, Stefan and Alex left and agreed to meet Haris at 3 in the afternoon in front of the main circus entrance. When the boys got there, people were already lining up waiting for the circus to start. It seemed like the whole town was there. They set their bikes carefully one on top of the other on the ground and got in line.

They were there for about five minutes when a group of clowns came running out of the tent and into the parking lot. They started doing all kinds of fun stuff. They were jumping, doing cartwheels, somersaults, and bouncing on pogo sticks. Then, one of them said something that made Haris, Stefan, and

Alex not believe their own ears.

He shouted, "We need some volunteers to do a balancing act! C'mon out here boys and girls; let's all walk the parking lot lines like they are tight ropes! We'll teach you. Lessons are free, c'mon, c'mon! This is the opportunity you have been waiting for! Come perform with the clowns! Come! Come!"

Before anyone else had a chance to respond, Haris yelled out, "We already know how to do this on our bikes!"

All the clowns' heads turned in the direction of the boys. All the clowns' eyes got bigger, all the clowns' eyebrows went up, and all the clowns' painted mouths and jaws dropped.

"What?" responded the head clown. "On your bikes?"

Then all the white-gloved clown hands pointed to the parking lot lines. The boys understood the clowns' silent command and ran to their bikes. They grabbed them and walked to one of the white lines. They stood one behind the other and waited. One of the clowns put a long silver whistle between his lips and blew loudly. Haris went first, then Alex, then Stefan. They rode the parking lot line as straight and as balanced as any real circus performer could have done. They went far from the crowd before they turned around and came back. Everyone's eyes were on them. People were clapping and shouting,

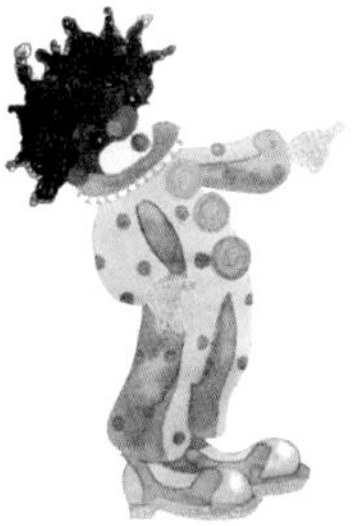

"Bravo! Bravo! Great act! Great act!"

The clowns were doing somersaults and cartwheels around them, blowing their whistles. The crowd was cheering them on. Haris, Stefan and Alex felt famous that afternoon, and they loved it.

It was time for the real show. Everyone went into the circus tent where the magic was about to begin. And magic it was! The show was the best the boys had ever seen. When it was over they rode back leisurely, talking all the way.

"What an afternoon!" Stefan said.

"Do you believe it?" Said Alex. "We were entertaining the crowd! We were part of the circus!"

"When the real wire act was going on, I was imagining I was already grown up and was the one riding up there," said Haris. "Why not? I could if I wanted to," he added with poise.

"We all can do it when we grow up if we want to," replied Stefan.

"Only if we decide to," said Alex. "If we choose to do it, we can do it. We know how to do all that stuff now."

13

BeJoWiLo's House

They rode in silence for a little while. BeJoWiLo and the events of the last few days were still crystal-clear in their minds. Haris spoke first.

"Alex, did you focus on something?" he asked.

"Yeah, did you change anything? You didn't tell us yet," said Stefan.

"I'm still doing it," said Alex. "I'm not ready to tell you guys yet. I will pretty soon, when I change it all the way."

"What is it?" they asked.

"Tell us now, we want to know now," said Stefan.

"No, not yet. I almost got it, I'm almost there," said Alex.

"When then?" asked Stefan.

"Maybe in a coupla days," replied Alex.

They reached the turn in the road where they had to go different directions. When the boys separated for the evening, they took with them loads of fun thoughts from the circus. But Stefan and Haris took a few more of a different kind. They took thoughts of curiosity and anticipation about Alex' project for change. But for now, all they could do was wait. Alex would tell them about his accomplishment when he was ready.

Haris was very happy that night. Lying in bed, thoughts of his accomplishment, the parking lot act, the doors, the gifts, the lessons, BeJoWiLo and her appearances were dancing in his head. The day's cheerful memories were surrounding him tenderly. Sinking into sleep, he whispered,

"BeJoWiLo, where do you live?"

Then he drifted into night travel. BeJoWiLo soon came and responded to his question. Gracefully and gently she explained where her house was. She said the mind was like a two story house, and that she lived in the upper house, while Haris lived in the lower house.

She also said it was easy to reach her anytime.

"Do I call on you like I did the other day?" Haris asked in the dream.

She said he could do that. He could call her down below when he was awake, or he could go meet her in the upper house in his dreams if he wanted to.

"What if you're not there? Do you ever leave?" he asked. Her explanation was simple. She said she was always home, mostly in the upper house. She also said never to forget that, because knowing it made it easier to contact her. Their dream conversation was comforting to Haris, and he remembered it word for word the next morning.

"I can't wait to tell Stefan and Alex all the things she said this time," Haris whispered, jumping out of bed.

He was excited knowing where BeJoWiLo was at all times. Either in the lower or in the upper house, it didn't matter. She was there to help and guide him with her wise and gentle suggestions.

This new friendship made Haris feel powerful, full of enthusiasm and belief that he was capable of many more achievements.

"I wonder if all people have a friend like BeJoWiLo in their upper house?" he mumbled softly. The question was repeating itself in his mind as he walked into the kitchen. Eating his breakfast didn't make it go away. He really wanted to know the answer. *Aha!* he thought with a mouthful of cereal. *I'm gonna find out tonight. I'll ask BeJoWiLo.*

The End.

About the Author

Demetra Yuvanu was born and raised in Athens, Greece. Through many life experiences in Athens, Turkey, Texas, Washington State, California and North Carolina, she now calls South Carolina, USA, home.

She is a mother of two sons and grandmother of two gorgeous boys! She is a certified Nia instructor, an Ageless Grace Educator, an EFT coach, an experiential workshop facilitator and the author of two books regarding choice, focus and manifestation, principles she has studied and has been applying all her adult life.

Demetra is passionate about Nia, which was love at first step and first sound 13 plus years ago in San Diego, CA. Dancing is her medicine.

A closer look: She gets excited about all things unique. Appreciates kindness and generosity. Gets nourished by spiritual wisdom. Enjoys indie films. Aims at bypassing trivialities and getting to the core. Comes alive when she's by the sea. Finds great fulfillment in inspiring others to open their wings and fly. Swimming is her other medicine. Gets excited refinishing and repurposing furniture that might appear useless to most. Really, really likes pistachio ice cream. Looks forward to meeting new authentic souls. Loves refrigerated figs. Loses interest quickly in superficial talk. Time stands still for her while doing yardwork.

Demetra loves engaging in juicy conversations, making warm connections, establishing unpretentious friendships and devoting herself to creative endeavors that nurture her soul.

She has also self published: *About Spiritual Mind Treatments*: *Setting the Law of Attraction in Motion;* A small book for big people.

Made in the USA
Middletown, DE
27 September 2019